THE SPY FIVE
OPERATION NIGHT FRIGHT

by Spencer Strange

with

Andrea Menotti ← words

and

Kelly Kennedy → pictures

Scholastic Inc.

New York Toronto London Auckland Sydney
Mexico City New Delhi Hong Kong Buenos Aires

Visit the Spy Five web site at
www.scholastic.com/spyfive

Your new password is:
spybynight

Stop by and send the Spy Five an e-mail. We love to hear from you!

Use this password to access a new game!

ISBN 0-439-70355-7

Copyright © 2005 by Scholastic Inc.

Design: Julie Mullarkey Gnoy

12 11 10 9 8 7 6 5 4 3 2 1   5 6 7 8 9/0

Printed in the U.S.A.

First printing, April 2005

CHAPTERS

CHAPTER 1
THANKS TO ANIKA

I don't know if you remember or not, but my dad was SUPPOSED to take me to Florida for my spring break. We were SUPPOSED to go there for a whole week and hit all the amusement parks. I'd been looking forward to it for a LONG TIME.

But you know what? As it turned out, there was some kind of big scientific conference in Chicago the same week as my spring break, so Dad CANCELLED the whole trip. In case you haven't guessed by all the capital letters, I was pretty MAD about it. And I still am.

IT'S A VERY IMPORTANT CONFERENCE. I'M PRESENTING MY RESEARCH...

You see, my dad spends *all* his time on his work. He just got back from a couple of months of research in Antarctica (of all places), so the Florida trip was supposed to be our chance to catch up. But instead he decided he just *had* to go to some dumb conference on "dark matter."

If you're wondering what "dark matter" is, you're not alone. Because NOBODY KNOWS. My dad's an astrophysicist, and he studies it. It's not like bright matter (like stars), which we can see. It's invisible. And it's everywhere. Dad says there's much, much more dark matter than bright matter in the universe.

But nobody knows what dark matter is made of, so a lot of people (like my dad) are trying to find out. They're kind of in a race. A big scientific race to figure out the mystery of dark matter. It's a very important matter, according to my dad.

But not to me.

Personally, I think there are other matters that are more important.

But that's just me.

Anyway, my dad tried to get my mom to let me go to Florida the week *before* my spring break or maybe the week *after*. But

Mom said it was *not* okay to take me out of school for a week to go on a vacation just 'cause it fit better with Dad's schedule. I said I'd make up all the work I missed, but Mom wouldn't budge. So I ended up with no Florida at all. Pretty depressing.

But wait, before you feel sorry for me, there was *also* good news that I found out about right after the bad news about Florida. And that good news was all thanks to Anika.

✳ ✳ ✳ ✳

"We're *in*, guys!" Anika said excitedly one Monday morning. "Copper Beech has an opening the first week of May!"

"We're going to the BEACH?" Ursula blasted.

"No, Copper *Beech*," Anika said. "As in beech *tree*. It's a kind of camp that kids go to with their schools for nature stuff like horseback riding and campfires. Remember I was telling you about it a couple months ago?"

"Oh yeah!" Blitz said. "That was the trip you were saying we could maybe do if our field trip with Mr. Lipsky went okay."

"Yup, that's the one," Anika said. "My mom and some other moms have been pushing for it for a while now, and we finally got an opening 'cause some other school cancelled. And since Mr. Naulty lifted the field-trip ban, thanks to our handiwork, our school gets to go!"

"The *whole* school?" Julian asked.

"No, just a hundred kids," Anika said. "But don't worry—my mom'll make sure that all of us are in."

"Sweet!" Julian said.

"Definitely," I chimed in.

"This is the best news I've heard in a *long* time," Ursula added.

"You said it," Blitz agreed. "I can't wait to get outta here!"

And then Blitz turned to Anika and said the words we all were thinking:

"You ROCK!"

That night at home, I got my mom to sign my permission slip. I showed her the Copper Beech brochure, and she was real impressed with the place. She even joked about coming along. But fortunately she was only kidding.

"You know," Mom added, "I think that's the week your father was going to try to visit."

"Too bad," I said with a shrug. "I'm not gonna be around."

It felt very good to say that. VERY good.

"All right," Mom said. "I'll let him know."

Good. Dad *definitely* deserved a taste of his own medicine, as far as I was concerned.

✳ ✳ ✳ ✳

After we got our permission slips in, we had a big meeting one night to talk about the trip. Everyone's parents were there, and so were all the teachers who were going.

Luckily, Mr. Naulty wasn't going (YES!). But Miss Pryor was going, and so were Mr. Lipsky and Mrs. Atticus. It was really funny to imagine them all decked out in camping gear, riding horses and stuff.

Mrs. Atticus

Miss Pryor

Mr. Lipsky

Anyway, once we got the details all squared away, it was just a matter of waiting through one more week of school, then spring break, and then camp was right after that.

Since Dad cancelled our Florida trip, I was going to spend my spring break with my grandma in Vermont. NOT EXACTLY A WEEK IN SUNNY FLORIDA. But since I knew I had camp to look forward to the week after, it was no big deal at all.

me in Vermont
for spring break

CHAPTER 2
OFF TO THE BEECH

It was about a two-hour drive from the city up to Camp Copper Beech in upstate New York. We drove there in yellow school buses (four of them), like the kind I rode to school every day when I lived in Maryland.

When we pulled into the camp, I knew right away that I was going to like the place. It had plenty of lawn space for sports, which was something I really missed from when I lived in Maryland (where I had my own yard).

And just like the picture in the brochure, there were horses standing around in the field beside the road. We saw them as we drove in. They didn't pay much

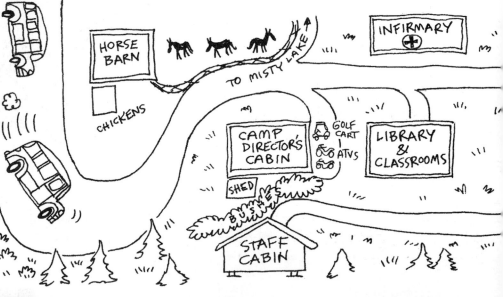

attention to us, but everyone on my bus started going nuts. Including Ursula. I had no idea she was such a big horse fan.

The camp also had lots of cool-looking buildings that were kind of like log cabins but more modern, with huge windows and tall ceilings. There were all sorts of signs pointing to places that looked interesting, like Willow Pond, Misty Lake, and Sunset Circle. And then there was a HUGE tree in the middle of all the buildings, which I knew from the brochure was the copper beech tree that the camp was named after. The bus pulled up right beside the tree.

Everyone was really excited as we piled off the bus. We were talking, laughing, and making all kinds of noise, but then suddenly everyone realized they'd better put a cork in it. And fast. Because *somebody* was looking at us with icy cold eyes.

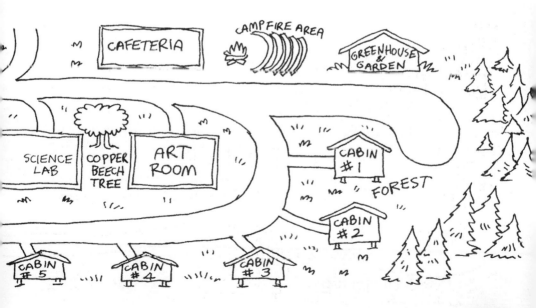

And that somebody turned out to be:

MR. STARK

People like Mr. Naulty had to do a lot of yelling to make everyone get quiet like that. But Mr. Stark just had to stand there and stare at us.

His face looked like it had permanent grumpy lines etched into it, and his clothes looked like they were from a hundred years ago. I couldn't even *guess* how old he was.

"Welcome to Camp Copper Beech," he said in a not-very-welcoming voice, like he'd said it a thousand times before. "I'm Mr. Stark, the camp director. You probably won't be seeing too much of me this week, because most of my work is behind the scenes. You'll be spending most of your time with my staff, who are waiting to meet you in your cabins. But you WILL see me if the need arises. Can anyone tell me when the need might arise?"

Everyone was silent. All you could hear was the sound of the copper beech tree blowing in the wind. Finally Ursula spoke up.

"If there's an emergency?" Ursula asked.

"Yes," Mr. Stark said. "If there's an emergency, I will be involved. Can anyone tell me *another* situation when I would need to be involved?"

Everyone was *really* quiet. I think we all knew what he was trying to get at, but no one wanted to be the one to say it.

"No one knows?" Mr. Stark asked again. "That's surprising."

"If there's any...trouble?" someone said from the back of the crowd.

"That's right," Mr. Stark said. "We have some very simple rules around here, which your counselors will tell you about. If you follow them, you'll have a great time this week. But if anyone has trouble following them, then you'll be seeing me. Is that understood?"

"Yes," everyone kind of mumbled. I hated it when people made us answer in unison like that, and I think everyone else did, too.

"Can't hear you," Mr. Stark said, holding his hand up to his ear.

"**YES!**" we all blasted out.

"That's what I like to hear," Mr. Stark said. "Now, can anyone tell me what kind of tree we're standing in front of?"

I knew, but I didn't say anything. A couple of people, including the teachers, said:

"A copper beech."

"That's right," Mr. Stark said. "That's the copper beech that this camp is named after. Can anyone guess how old it is?"

Nobody had any idea, and nobody wanted to sound stupid by guessing wrong. So Mr. Stark finally had to answer his own question.

"About two hundred years old," he said. "Two centuries old. That's a long time, isn't it?"

Again, there was just silence and the sound of wind blowing through leaves.

"You'll walk past this tree many times a day while you're here," Mr. Stark continued. "And each time you do, think about how long it's been standing right there in that spot, how much it's seen and endured. It deserves our greatest respect."

Mr. Stark paused for a moment and turned to look at the tree. I wondered if he was getting all misty-eyed. But then he turned back around and changed the subject.

"So," he said, "that's our tree. *Now* it's time for your orientation. Your teachers have lists of the cabin assignments. When you hear your name called, please take your bag and stand behind your teacher. Quietly. Then you'll walk up to the cabins together."

"This is like *military* school," Julian mumbled as we waited for our names to be called.

"It'll get better, guys," Anika whispered. "They just lay down the law first, then we have fun."

"Hope so," Blitz whispered.

Yeah, no kidding.

✳ ✳ ✳ ✳

Fortunately, the cabin assignments were exactly what we were hoping for. All the guys in our grade were in the same cabin (Cabin 5), so Blitz, Julian, and I were all together. Ursula and Anika were together, too, in Cabin 4, right next door.

Stefan

When we got to our cabin, we met our cabin counselor, Stefan. We were all relieved 'cause he seemed a hundred percent cooler than Mr. Stark. Stefan knew how to smile, at least. *And* he said he knew some great ghost stories, which sounded like fun.

It wasn't *all* good news, though. Every cabin had one teacher assigned to it, and unfortunately, we got Mr. Lipsky, our science teacher. As you might remember from *Operation Master Mole*, Mr. Lipsky is famous around school for flossing his teeth at his desk and spraying between-the-teeth crud all over the place. So no one

Mr. Lipsky

was too pleased to find out we were stuck with him. But at least he had his own room and his own bathroom, so hopefully he'd keep his flossing to himself. But of course we could never be sure.

Stefan took us on a tour of our cabin. Besides the usual stuff like bunk beds and bathrooms, the cabin had lots of fun stuff, like a sitting area with beanbag chairs, some games, and even some books, which I couldn't imagine anyone would actually take the time to read. But it was a nice thought.

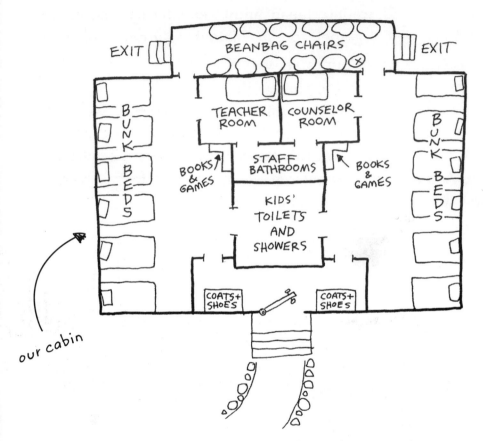

our cabin

After we'd all picked out our bunks and put our bags on the shelves, it was time to head back to the dining hall for the whole-group orientation. So we all walked outside and waited on the steps till everyone was ready.

And that's when my friend Sohail (from my silent reading class) made his discovery.

"ATVs!" he yelled, pointing toward the director's cabin, which was just down the way from us.

Sohail

ATVs!

"What are ATVs?" a couple of people asked, looking in the distance.

"All-terrain vehicles!" Sohail explained, practically jumping up and down with excitement. "See! There are two!"

And sure enough, there were two ATVs parked in the director's driveway. They looked really cool. There was also a golf cart there, but no one really paid any attention to that.

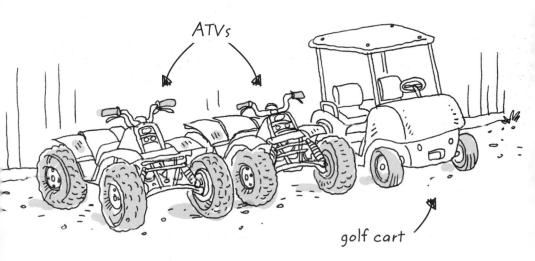

ATVs

golf cart

I knew why Sohail was so excited. You see, he's totally obsessed with motorcycles. He's always drawing them. Every model you can imagine. He even says he's *driven* motorcycles before (on some banana farm in Yemen, the country where he's from). So, considering his obsession with motorcycles, it made sense that he'd be into ATVs, too.

"Cool," Julian agreed. "Do you think we get to ride 'em, like the horses?"

"YEAH!" Blitz cheered.

Sohail turned and asked Stefan excitedly, "Can we ride the ATVs?"

"Oh, no," Stefan said. "I've been here for a year, and I've *never* had a ride on one of those. Mr. Stark's pretty much the only one who ever rides 'em."

"What's he use 'em for?" Sohail asked.

"Dunno," Stefan said with a shrug. "I think he takes them hunting and off-roading. And he'd use them if there was ever an emergency out on the trails. But for the most part, he just uses that golf cart around the camp."

"HE HAS TWO ATVs AND HE DRIVES A GOLF CART?" Sohail demanded, totally shocked.

"Yup," Stefan said.

"That's like having two BMWs and driving an old-lady car!" Sohail said in shock.

"You *said* it," Julian agreed.

"Hey, I'm with you," Stefan said with a shrug. "But Mr. Stark is...Mr. Stark. He's not like most people."

That was for sure.

Sohail shook his head in disbelief as we all walked down to the dining hall.

"Man," he said. "If I thought Mr. Stark was weird before, I *definitely* think he's weird now."

When we got to the dining hall, the girls were already there. Anika was chatting with her friends, like usual. But Ursula was standing in front of the fireplace, staring at the giant deer head that was hanging above it. Her eyebrows were all knit together, so I knew something was wrong. Julian, Blitz, and I went over to see her.

"What's wrong?" I asked.

"Mr. Stark killed this deer," Ursula said. "And then he chopped off its head and hung it on the wall!"

We were all silent.

"Don't people do that kind of thing when they hunt?" Blitz asked. "I saw it on TV—"

"BUT WHAT DID THE POOR DEER EVER DO TO DESERVE THIS?" Ursula interrupted. "Its head is hanging on a *wall*, people."

Everyone was silent again.

"Have you turned into a vegetarian or something?" Julian asked.

"No," Ursula said. "But I don't believe in killing wild animals like it's some kind of sport."

"I'm with Ursula," Anika said, walking up to us right then. "That poor deer got no respect."

"And you know what ELSE the cabin counselor told me?" Ursula asked.

"What?" we all asked.

"She said that when Mr. Stark kills a deer, they make DEER MEAT CHILI for everyone at the camp."

"DEER MEAT CHILI?!" we all shouted at once.

That was just *too* gross.

But before we could hear any more gory deer meat details, Mr. Stark walked in, everyone got quiet, and the rest of our orientation began. We all sat at one of the dining hall tables and listened as Mr. Stark went over the hundred thousand million rules they have around Camp Copper Beech. But the whole time, I wasn't thinking about the rules.

I was thinking about Mr. Stark, wondering what his story was, and what I was going to find out about him during our week at Copper Beech.

Something told me it was going to be interesting....

As it turned out, it got interesting almost right away. After our orientation, we had some free time in our cabins before dinner. Everyone did their own thing:

- Julian, Blitz, and I played card games.

- Sohail sat on the steps of our cabin and drew one of Mr. Stark's ATVs.

- Anika hung out in the hammocks outside the cabins with her friends.

• And Ursula read some of the books in her cabin library.

If you thought Ursula's choice was the most boring, think again. Because Ursula was the one who made the big discovery that started our whole investigation.

She was *really* excited about it. She came running into the dining hall to show it to us before dinner.

"GUYS!" she said, her eyes all enormous. "You won't *believe* what I found in this book!"

And she showed us a book called *Animals of the Northeast Woodlands*.

"You actually READ one of the books in the cabin?" Julian asked in shock.

"I was *trying* to find out what kinds of animals we might see this week," Ursula said. "But then I found *this*!"

And she pulled out a note and showed it to us:

To the kids who stay here after us,

We heard a weird voice coming from Mr. Stark's cabin one night. It sounded like a woman's voice, real high-pitched. It said:
GOTTA GET OUTTA HERE!

We are freaked out. TOTALLY.
We think it might have something to do with Mr. Stark's mother.

But we're not sure.

Just warning you. Stay safe.
Don't go out at night. And keep an eye on Mr. Stark. He's weird.

- Evan, Taylor, Jordan, and Darcy

"They stayed here last month," Ursula said. "See the date on the back? So this stuff just happened!"

"Whoa," Anika said. "That's *freaky*!"

The rest of us were still trying to figure out what exactly to make of the note.

"Mr. Stark has a *mother*?" Blitz asked, his eyes wide.

"EVERYONE HAS A MOTHER!" we all said at once.

"I mean a mother who's still *alive*," Blitz said.

"Yeah," Anika agreed. "That guy seems ancient."

"Like he's from the Stone Age," I added.

"I guess we'll have to ask around and see what we can find out," Anika said.

"*And* listen around Mr. Stark's cabin and see what we hear," I added.

Everyone kind of shivered. But they all nodded.

"I've had a *baaaad* feeling about that guy since we first stepped off the bus," Julian said.

"Me too," I agreed.

"I hope it's nothing awful," Anika said. "This week was supposed to be fun."

"Well, it might just be a joke," Ursula said. "Those kids might just be trying to freak people out, you know."

"That's true," Anika said. "People *do* tell a lot of ghost stories around here, so maybe they were just trying their own scare tactics."

That *was* a possibility...but I had a funny feeling those kids weren't messing around.

After we ate our dinner (which was fried chicken, fortunately— *not* deer meat chili), we went outside for a campfire. It was a real campfire, like the kind you see in the movies. We even got to roast marshmallows on sticks. It was so cool, I actually stopped thinking about the freaky letter.

But not for long.

Because Mr. Stark showed up.

At first I didn't even notice he was there. I just noticed that

the kids around me suddenly got quieter, and a lot of people were looking over at the shadowy area beyond the fire. Then I looked over there and saw, just barely, Mr. Stark standing in the shadows, watching all of us. Finally he stepped forward into the light, took a seat on a tree stump, and started another one of his speeches.

"As I mentioned when we first met, you probably won't be seeing much of me for the rest of your stay," Mr. Stark said in a quiet voice. "But I wanted to take this opportunity to tell you a little story about our copper beech tree...and about someone who came a long way to see it."

Ugh! *More talk about that tree? Enough already! I think* everyone else had the same thought.

But Mr. Stark continued.

"I first heard this story about fifty years ago," Mr. Stark said, his voice getting even quieter, "when I was a boy. My family owned a farm very near this land, so I knew this tree quite well. I first saw it when I was five years old, and it made a big impression on me. And when I first heard the story of Jake Magorty when I was ten, it made a big impression on me, too. I found it quite...*startling.*"

Then Mr. Stark paused and turned to the counselors, who were sitting on their own tree stumps behind him, and asked:

"Didn't you find the story startling when you first heard it?"

"Oh, yes," Stefan said with wide eyes. "*Very* startling."

"It's a real shocker," another counselor agreed, looking very serious.

And suddenly we were all very interested in hearing this story. So we all leaned in and listened closely as Mr. Stark began, in a quiet voice...

This story takes place around the turn of the twentieth century, back when our tree was a hundred years old. Even then, it was already majestic, known and admired by many... including one person who had never actually seen it. His name was Jake Magorty.

Jake Magorty was an old man. Very old. And he was not very well. His left leg had been injured in the Civil War, so he walked with a limp and was always in pain. By the time he was eighty, he could hardly walk from one side of his little house to the other.

He lived about a mile north of here, in a small town on the other side of the forest. He spent most of his time sitting on a

rocking chair on his porch, wearing the little green cap he was never seen without, talking to anyone who passed. He had no family, so he was entirely alone, except for the kind neighbors who stopped by to chat and bring him food.

Mr. Magorty loved to talk about the trees he could see from his porch, and how they changed from summer to fall to winter to spring. He loved nature's beauty with all his heart.

He had heard talk of the beautiful copper beech on the other side of the forest, but he'd never seen it with his own eyes. He often said he wished he had gone to see it back when he still could. Now the walk was much too far for him.

One of the neighbors who came to see him on occasion was a boy about your age. His name was Sam. Sam's mother would send him to Mr. Magorty's house with jars of applesauce, bowls of mashed potatoes, and other soft foods and soups. Since Mr. Magorty had almost no teeth left, that was just about all he could eat.

But one day when Sam arrived with a jar of pea soup, Mr. Magorty was not on his rocking chair. And Mr. Magorty's cane was nowhere in sight. Sam knocked on the door, but Mr. Magorty did not call out to answer. Sam even opened the door (since it was always unlocked) and looked inside the house, fearing the worst. But Mr. Magorty was nowhere to be found.

So Sam went back outside and looked around. In the distance, he could just barely make out the tiny form of Mr. Magorty hobbling down the road toward the forest. He knew it was Mr. Magorty because he recognized the bright green cap. No one else wore a cap like that.

Sam called to Mr. Magorty and ran down the road to catch up. When he found Mr. Magorty, the old man was clearly in a lot of pain. He was wincing and out of breath.

"Where are you going, Mr. Magorty?" Sam asked.

"To the copper beech tree," Mr. Magorty said. "I've decided that the time has finally come for me to see it. Will you help me make it through the forest?"

"But Mr. Magorty," Sam protested, "if you really want to go, we can have someone give you a ride on a wagon, or—"

"No, no, I have to walk," Mr. Magorty interrupted. "Will you please help me?"

Sam couldn't possibly refuse such a heartfelt request, so he agreed. He walked slowly alongside Mr. Magorty on the path through the forest, holding his arm to keep him steady. Sam couldn't even imagine how long it was going to take to walk a full mile to the copper beech tree. It was already late afternoon, and soon the sun would be starting to set. But Sam was so impressed with Mr. Magorty's strong will, he felt he had to help him, no matter how long it took.

Then something amazing happened. As the sun began to set, Mr. Magorty suddenly handed his cane to Sam.

"I don't think I need this anymore," he said. "My leg feels brand-new!"

"Really?" Sam asked in amazement, taking the cane from Mr. Magorty. "The walk must have done you good!"

"It certainly has!" Mr. Magorty agreed, picking up his pace. "How wonderful to walk freely again!"

"And how lucky that we'll make it to the tree before sunset now," Sam added.

"Indeed!" Mr. Magorty said.

Sam knew how impressive the tree was, so he was glad that Mr. Magorty was going to be able to see it in all its glory before it got too dark. Sam knew the forest path quite well, and he knew the tree was close.

But then another amazing thing happened, even more amazing than before: Mr. Magorty suddenly started to run!

"Mr. Magorty!" Sam called, running to catch up. "Are you sure you're all right?"

"Oh yes!" Mr. Magorty said with a great big smile. "I feel better than I have in years!"

Mr. Magorty kept running, and Sam ran right alongside him, till finally they reached the clearing where the copper beech tree stood in the middle.

"AHHHH!" Mr. Magorty gasped when he reached the clearing. "There it is! It's as beautiful as I imagined! And more!"

Mr. Magorty stared at the tree with a look of absolute joy on his face.

"I feel like...I could fly!" Mr. Magorty said.

And then he started to run again.

"Be careful, Mr. Magorty!" Sam called. "Don't—"

But before Sam could finish speaking, he saw Mr. Magorty lift off the ground and fly toward the top of the tree like a bird...

"THIS ISN'T A TRUE STORY!" someone suddenly interrupted. It felt like a spell had been broken. I couldn't believe someone would actually interrupt *Mr. Stark* of all people.

"SHHH!" everyone else said.

"Now hold on a moment," Mr. Stark said. "I'm telling you what Sam *said* he saw. He always swore that he'd really seen Mr. Magorty take off and fly to the top of the tree. You can believe it or not believe it. Your choice."

Of course, *that* set off a huge wave of responses:

Finally Mr. Stark interrupted.

"Well, if you all want to sit here and debate, we don't have to finish the story," Mr. Stark said, rising from his tree stump.

"NO!" everyone protested. **"FINISH THE STORY!"**

So Mr. Stark sat back down and continued. His voice got real quiet again.

...Sam watched in shock as Mr. Magorty flew to the top of the tree, did one complete circle around it, and then disappeared behind the branches.

When Mr. Magorty didn't reappear, Sam ran around the back of the tree to look for him. But he wasn't there. Sam even ran under the tree and looked up into the branches. But it was getting dark, so he couldn't see much at all.

MR. MAGORTY!

"Mr. Magorty!" Sam called.

No answer.

Finally Sam stepped out from under the tree and looked around the clearing.

And that's when he saw a small dark heap in the grass, right where he'd seen Mr. Magorty take off into flight. Sam gasped and went running toward it.

And sure enough, there was Mr. Magorty, lying in the grass. He looked happy and peaceful and...

...he was dead.

Mr. Stark paused right then and got up from his stump.

"Is that the end?" someone asked.

"Oh, no," Mr. Stark said, shaking his head. "Trust me—you'll know when I've reached the end."

Then Mr. Stark took a deep breath and continued:

"Mr. Magorty's neighbors wanted to bury him near the copper beech tree he loved so much, but they didn't want to risk disturbing the tree's root system. So they buried him a little ways away, quite close to where we're sitting, actually—"

"**WHERE?**" everyone demanded.

"I don't know exactly where, because the grave was unmarked," Mr. Stark said. "But I know it's near here. Maybe it's right under my feet...or *yours*."

Some of the girls squealed and lifted their feet off the ground.

"And *some* say that on certain nights, if you listen very closely to the forest, you can hear the sound Mr. Magorty made when he first stepped out into the clearing and saw the tree. Like this: *"AHHHH!"*

"You mean you can hear his *ghost*?" someone asked.

"I suppose you could call it that," Mr. Stark said. "Let's listen now."

We all listened. It was dead quiet.

"I don't hear anything," some people said.

"Yeah, me neither," others agreed.

"I guess Mr. Magorty's not roaming about the forest tonight," Mr. Stark said with a shrug. "But I must say, I'm not surprised."

"Why not?" someone asked.

"Well, because *usually* when I tell this story, he likes... TO LISTEN!"

And right when he said that, Mr. Stark flipped on his flashlight and shined it on the ground in the darkness beyond the fire. And there we saw, to our horror...

MR. MAGORTY'S HEAD STICKING OUT OF THE GROUND!

Of course, everyone jumped a mile and screamed bloody murder. *I* even jumped, and *I'd* seen it coming. Well, sort of.

Mr. Stark laughed. And the counselors all laughed, too.

"GOTCHA!" Mr. Stark yelled, still chuckling.

"We *told* you it'd be shocking," Stefan said.

Everyone was still catching their breath.

"**YOU!**" people yelled, because they didn't know what else to say. Most people were laughing, but not everyone.

"I'm gonna have nightmares now!" some girl said.

"It's just a *story!*" someone yelled back. "He wasn't a real person!"

"I *knew* it was fake!" someone else yelled.

"It was *still* scary!" the nightmare girl insisted.

"Don't be scared," Mr. Stark said, picking up the head and the arm. "This is just a bunch of plastic. Bought it off the internet—"

"Not funny!" the nightmare girl muttered.

Well, I guess you can't please everyone.

But *I* for one thought it was a real good scare.

CHAPTER 4
GOTTA GET OUTTA HERE!

After the Jake Magorty story, we were all convinced that the kids who stuck the freaky note in Ursula's book were just trying to pull off their own scare. We figured they'd probably heard the Magorty story, too, so they must've wanted to get in on the horror-story action. But we weren't buying it. No way.

So we went about our business at Camp Copper Beech and had a great time the next two days.

There were all kinds of classes you could take, and they let you pick the ones you wanted (so you weren't forced into anything boring). I took art classes every day in this really cool building that had every art supply you could imagine. I did lots of "still-life" drawings of natural stuff, like this one:

STILL LIFE WITH DEER DROPPINGS

deer droppings

We took hikes in the forest and learned how to use compasses and the sun to figure out which way was which. Well, sort of.

We planted watermelon and cantaloupe seeds in the greenhouse and helped get the garden ready for the spring growing season.

We fed the chickens and collected their eggs, which were brown, not white. (And Ursula knew why, surprise surprise.)

And, of course, we got to ride horses. We rode on the trail around the lake, which was very cool. But you wouldn't believe how much horses have to—*ahem*—do their business. It was pretty gross. When they say horses eat a *lot*, they're not kidding.

* * * *

One thing that *no one* expected was that Sohail actually managed to sneak over to Mr. Stark's place to check out his ATVs. Now *that* was bold, considering Mr. Stark's cabin was totally off-limits to kids, and his ATVs were even *more* off-limits.

But still, one afternoon, Sohail decided to take a walk over to get a closer look at the precious ATVs. And then he got a little bolder and walked a little closer. And closer. And then he was standing right in front of one of them, and no one was around, so he went even farther: He climbed into the driver's seat!

Of course, he didn't have the key, so he didn't turn the thing on, but he said it was still cool to see all the controls. He told me, Julian, and Blitz all about it when he came back. We were all hanging out in the cabin during our free time before dinner.

"It was so cool, guys," he said. "I could *totally* drive that thing if they'd let me."

"Good luck," I said.

"I know," Sohail said, rolling his eyes.

"Can we go look at it with you tomorrow?" Julian asked.

"Yeah!" Blitz agreed.

"I don't know," Sohail said, looking hesitant. "I don't think I want to go back there."

And then he paused and added:

"It was kind of creepy over there, you know."

"Why?" I asked.

I HEARD SOME.... WEIRD STUFF.

"I heard some...weird stuff," Sohail said.

"Like what?" Julian asked.

"Well, I heard someone inside Mr. Stark's house say, 'Gotta get outta here.'"

When I heard *that*, my eyes just about fell out of my head. I looked over at Julian and Blitz, and they looked the same.

"YOU DID?!" we all asked.

"Yeah," Sohail said. "And then I heard Mr. Stark's voice say 'shut up!' And then the other person said 'shut up!' right back at him!"

"REALLY?" we all said, our eyes even wider than before.

"Yeah," Sohail said. "It was like a fight."

"What else did they say?" I asked.

"I don't know," Sohail said. "'Cause when I heard Mr. Stark's voice, I jumped off the ATV and started running back here. He sounded real mad, and I wasn't gonna stick around to get caught."

"Good move," Blitz said.

"Who do you think the other person was?" I asked.

"I don't know," Sohail said. "I thought Stefan said Mr. Stark lived alone and really liked his privacy."

"That's what *I* heard, too," Julian agreed.

"What did the voice sound like?" I asked.

"Kind of high and whiny, like an old lady's voice, maybe," Sohail said. "And it sounded kind of muffled, too."

"Like the person's mouth was covered?" Julian asked.

"I *hope* not," Sohail said, looking at us like we were crazy. "You think Mr. Stark would hold someone captive in his cabin?"

"We don't know what to think," I said. "Sit with us at dinner, and we'll tell you what we've found out so far."

* * * *

At dinner, over plates of beef stew, we told Anika and Ursula about what Sohail had heard.

"You're KIDDING!" Ursula blasted. "Did you tell him about my note?"

"What note?" Sohail asked.

So Ursula explained about the note she'd found.

"We thought it was a joke," Ursula said, "but obviously it wasn't."

"Whoa—that's scary," Sohail said. "You think it really could be Mr. Stark's *mother*?"

We all shrugged.

"That's just what those other kids thought," Ursula said. "We don't know what kind of evidence they were working with."

"Maybe his mother has to stay inside 'cause she's real old and can't walk or something," Blitz suggested. "But maybe she really wants to go out."

"Like Jake Magorty!" Julian said.

"Yeah," Blitz agreed.

"You *really* think he'd tell his mother to *shut up?*" Sohail asked.

It *did* sound really awful.

"Who *knows* what he's capable of," Ursula said.

"He *is* pretty creepy," Anika agreed. "I mean, who orders skeleton parts off the internet?"

"And who chops off a deer's head and hangs it on the wall?" Ursula chimed in. "And I'm *sure* that deer's not the only victim. Who *knows* how many other poor animals he's murdered."

"And made into chili," Blitz added.

Everyone shuddered.

"That's why we have to investigate. *Tonight,*" Ursula said firmly, dropping her fork on her plate with a big clunk.

One of the counselors sitting at the head of the table heard Ursula's fork go clunk and looked our way.

"Ursula, I told you, you have my *word* that's not venison," she said.

"Venison" is the official word for deer meat, in case you didn't know. (I didn't.)

"I know, I know," Ursula said. "I'm *eating*. I'm just resting."

After the counselor looked away, Ursula lowered her voice to a whisper and added:

"I think we should go listen outside Mr. Stark's cabin tonight. Just to see if we can hear *the voice.*"

"You're gonna go there at *night?*" Sohail asked with wide eyes.

"Better to go at night than in broad daylight," Ursula said with a shrug.

"Definitely," I agreed, and the rest of us nodded.

"And I have *just* the equipment for night spying," Blitz said excitedly.

"What?" we all asked.

"Headlamps with red lights," Blitz said. "They're perfect for night vision. I was saving 'em for the night hike tomorrow, but we can use them early."

"Sweet!" Julian said.

"Let's meet outside our cabin at 8:30, near the back porch," I suggested.

And so it was a plan.

I have to say, I had no idea what to expect for our night-spying operation. My imagination was coming up with all sorts of possibilities.

And most of them weren't very pretty.

CHAPTER 5
FELIX! FELIX!

That night, we had free time in our cabins after dinner to come up with our acts for the talent show we were having on Thursday. So that was the perfect time for us to slip out to Mr. Stark's cabin.

It was a pretty risky thing to do, because it involved breaking a bunch of the hundred thousand million rules Mr. Stark told us about at the beginning. Not *only* were Mr. Stark's cabin and the staff cabin off-limits to kids, but it was even *worse* to go there when we were supposed to be in our cabins for the night.

But fortunately, Mr. Lipsky always wanted people to go outside to look at the stars, so it wasn't like it would be tough to get out the door. And even *more* fortunately, there were bushes lining the path to Mr. Stark's cabin, so we had plenty of hiding places once we got out there.

Sohail even volunteered to stay behind and be a lookout for us. He said he'd give us a signal (a flashlight flash from the window) if anyone noticed we were gone.

And speaking of flashlights, it turned out that Blitz had brought along the *ultimate* night-spying lights. He'd designed and built them himself, as usual.

red and white lights

And what was especially cool was that he'd actually made *five* of them, one for each person in the Spy Five. Julian and I could hardly believe it when Blitz started unloading them from his bag.

"You built *five* of them?" I asked.

"Yup," Blitz said proudly. "I modeled them off this camping light my dad has. Except *his* light had only white light. I added red light 'cause it's much better for night vision."

"Why?" Julian asked.

"'Cause the red light helps your eyes stay adjusted to the dark, so you can still see okay after you turn the light off," Blitz explained. "If you use a bright white light, you have to wait for your eyes to adjust again before you can really see."

"Sweet!" Julian said, flipping the light between red and white. "Thanks, man."

"Yeah, thanks," I agreed, slipping the headlamp into my pocket.

Just then, Sohail came running up to us.

"Guys," he whispered, "the girls are out there already."

"Oh, snap!" Julian said. "It's 8:30 ALREADY?"

"No," Sohail said. "It's only 8:15. But they're out there. I saw 'em out the window. They're standing outside their cabin, talking or something."

"Guess they're ready to go," I said, kind of surprised that the girls would jump the gun like that. "You guys ready?"

"Yup," Julian and Blitz both nodded.

"Good luck," Sohail said. "I'll stay at the window till you guys get back."

"Thanks," we all said, quietly making our way to the door.

✳ ✳ ✳ ✳

Once we got outside, we all looked over toward the girls' cabin, and sure enough, Ursula and Anika were standing out there. There was light coming from their cabin window, so we could see them just fine without our headlamps.

But they didn't see *us*, because they were facing the other way, toward the cabin. And it looked like they were—if you can believe it—dancing.

Dancing at a time like this?

"What are they doing?" Blitz asked.

"Shhh," Julian and I both said, because we both had the same thought.

"Let's sneak up on them," Julian said with a grin.

So we tiptoed up behind the girls. Anika was counting out loud, doing a dance move with every beat. Ursula was trying to follow her, but she wasn't exactly doing a very good job of it.

"I keep forgetting that hop-hop thing," Ursula said, sounding frustrated.

"It's like this," Anika said, turning around to explain.

And that's when Anika saw us.

And that's *also* when I realized that we should have thought this through better, because it looked like Anika was gonna scream her lungs out.

But fortunately she caught herself just in time.

"You GUYS!" she whispered. "You scared me!"

And then Ursula turned and saw us, too.

"HEY!" she said. "How long have you been watching?"

"Long *enough*," Julian said with a smile.

Ursula glowered.

"You're not supposed to be here yet!" she whispered. "You're early!"

"What are you guys *doing*?" Blitz asked.

"We're practicing for the talent show," Anika explained. "I'm making up a dance routine for the whole cabin. We had to figure out a reason for me and Ursula to be outside, so I got permission to teach Ursula out here where it's quiet...kind of like a private lesson."

"Yeah, 'private' is the key word," Ursula said, glaring at Julian. "You shouldn't be creeping around in the dark SPYING on people."

"Hey, isn't that what we're *supposed* to be doing out here?" Julian asked.

"Yeah, not doing the 'hop-hop thing,'" Blitz agreed with a grin.

"But you're not supposed to spy on US!" Ursula argued.

"*Anyway,*" I said, changing the subject. "We should probably get going before someone hears us."

"Good point," Anika said. "Do we get stylin' forehead lights like yours?"

"Yup," Blitz said, handing the girls their headlamps. "They're just for emergencies, 'cause otherwise they'll make us too easy to spot."

"Gotcha," Anika said, taking her light. "Thanks for hooking us up!"

"No problem," Blitz said.

And so the girls put on their headlamps, and we were off.

There were no lights on in the staff cabin, and only one light in Mr. Stark's cabin, so it was *really* dark on that side of the camp. But fortunately our eyes were pretty adjusted to the dark already, so we didn't have too much trouble seeing.

When we got to Mr. Stark's cabin, it was dead quiet. The only room that had lights on was over on the *opposite* side of the cabin (lucky for us). So we figured we just had to keep real quiet so we didn't attract any attention.

We wanted to hide behind the bushes near the shed, but we didn't want to make too much noise by rustling around in there. So we took turns turning on our red lights and quietly moving through the branches and leaves till we found good spots to hide.

Once we were in our spots, we waited.

And waited.

And waited some more.

But there was no voice coming from Mr. Stark's cabin. After about fifteen or twenty minutes (which seemed like forever), I could tell everyone was starting to get real tired of waiting there in the dark.

But then, suddenly, we heard a rustling sound coming from the forest behind us. It was pitch black over there, so we had no idea what was making all that noise. And of course, we were fearing the worst. It sounded like something *big*. And it definitely sounded like it was coming our way.

"You think it's a deer?" Ursula whispered to me.

"Probably," I whispered back. "What else could it be?"

"A grizzly bear?" Julian asked.

Anika and Blitz gasped.

"There are no grizzly bears here," Ursula whispered. "Only black bears, and they don't attack people...*usually*."

"It's probably a deer," I said. "I mean, we've seen lots of deer in the forest, right?"

"Let's turn on the lights and look," Blitz suggested. "The *red* lights."

"Okay," I said, wanting to put the matter to rest.

Since we were looking in the opposite direction from Mr. Stark's house, it didn't seem like a big deal to turn on our lights.

So we all switched on our headlamps and looked...

And *here's* what we saw:

"EW! It's a RAT!" Anika gasped, covering her mouth.

It definitely looked like a rat—the world's *biggest* rat, to be exact. The thing was staring back at us, its eyes glowing red in our red light. Yech.

"That's SO nasty!" Julian whispered.

"OH, MAN!" Blitz gasped. "I didn't even know they *had* rats out here in the woods."

"That's not a rat!" Ursula suddenly insisted. "It's an opossum!"

"**A WHAT?**" we all said at the same time.

And suddenly the thing got freaked out and dashed back into the forest.

"An opossum. It's a *marsupial,* like a kangaroo. It keeps its babies in a pouch. And it hangs upside down by its—"

But just as Ursula was in the middle of explaining, we all heard something strange:

The sound of a car coming up the camp road.

"Lights off, guys!" I whispered.

And we all clicked off our lights and looked at the car moving slowly along the road in the distance.

We hadn't seen many cars our whole time at the camp, so it was weird to see this car all of a sudden. And the way the car was moving, it definitely seemed like the driver was lost.

"Wonder where *he's* going," I whispered.

And I guess someone *else* was asking that same question, because suddenly Mr. Stark's porch light came on, and the door opened, and out stepped Mr. Stark himself.

We all ducked as far down into the bushes as we could. And we held our breath.

Mr. Stark stood on his porch for a *very long* couple of seconds, looking down at the car on the road. Then finally he started walking down his driveway toward the car and (sigh of relief) *away* from us.

"Let's get out of here, guys," I whispered as soon as Mr. Stark was out of hearing range.

But just as I said those words, a strange, faint sound came out from the darkness behind Mr. Stark's open door:

"**FELIX!**"

And then we heard it again:

"**FELIX!**"

We all looked at one another with huge eyes.

"The voice!" Blitz whispered.

It was the strangest voice I'd ever heard—kind of high and whiny, just like Sohail had described it. Almost like a moan.

"Felix?" Ursula repeated. "Did she say 'Felix'?"

"I think so," Anika said.

"You think that's Mr. Stark's name?" Ursula asked.

"Maybe," I whispered.

I looked down at the road, and I saw that Mr. Stark was talking to the driver of the car. I started to imagine what might happen next: What if the car turned in to Mr. Stark's driveway and shined its headlights right on us? It seemed like it was *definitely* not a good idea to hang around there any longer.

And that's when we heard:

"GOTTA GET OUTTA HEEEEEEERE!"

The word "HERE" lasted a really long time, till it finally trailed off at the end. *Very* creepy. Everyone looked horrified.

And, as you can probably imagine, we didn't waste any time **getting outta there**.

CHAPTER 6
A STRANGE SURPRISE

"PHEW!" we all said when we made it safely back to the steps of Cabin 5.

"We'll talk to our counselor tonight and find out as much as we can about Mr. Stark," Anika volunteered.

"*And* his mother," Ursula added.

"We'll ask Stefan, too," I agreed.

And so the girls said good night and headed back to Cabin 4.

Once Julian, Blitz, and I were back inside our cabin, Sohail came rushing up to us.

"Nice escape," he said. "I saw Mr. Stark standing there on the porch, and I was *sure* he was gonna look your way."

"It was close," Julian agreed.

"So, didya hear *the voice*?" Sohail asked.

"*Oh* yeah," I said, nodding with big eyes.

"We heard 'Gotta get outta here!' just like you did. *And* we heard 'Felix!' a couple times, too," Julian said.

"*Felix*?" Sohail repeated. "Who's that?"

Julian and I both shrugged.

"That's what we're gonna try to figure—" I started to say, but then I heard:

"Spencer!"

And I looked up and saw Stefan walking toward us.

"Mr. Stark is at the door," he said. "He wants to speak to you."

My heart suddenly started pounding.

"*Me?*" I asked.

"Yup," Stefan said. "*You.* Unless there's another Spencer Strange I don't know about."

I swallowed hard.

"I'll come with you," Julian said.

"Me too," Blitz said, and Sohail agreed.

So we all walked out to the front door, where, sure enough, Mr. Stark was waiting for me. He looked as serious and stone-faced as ever.

"Which one of you's Spencer Strange?" he asked.

"Me," I said, taking a deep breath and stepping forward.

I was *sure* this had something to do with our expedition to Mr. Stark's cabin. I was *sure* we were busted. Had Mr. Stark seen us? Had someone told on us? But as it turned out, I was completely, totally, utterly wrong.

"*You* have a surprise visitor," Mr. Stark said, moving aside so someone *else* could step inside...

It was my dad.

I could hardly believe it.

"What are YOU doing here?" I asked.

"I wanted to see you," Dad said. "Your mom told me where you were, so I flew into New York, rented a car, and drove up here. Had a little trouble finding the place, though."

So DAD must've been the one driving the car we'd seen coming up the road!

"I can't *believe* you came all the way up here," I said, shaking my head.

"Well, why don't you invite your father inside?" Mr. Stark suggested.

"You're gonna *stay* here?" I asked, looking down at Dad's bag.

"Sure," Dad said, stepping inside.

"He'll be an extra chaperone in this cabin," Mr. Stark explained. "There's an extra bunk in the teacher's room."

So Dad was going to have to share a room with Mr. Lipsky? If I weren't still in complete shock, I might have actually found that funny.

✳ ✳ ✳ ✳

After Dad met all my friends and the other people in our cabin, he suggested we all go outside to check out the stars.

"It's a perfect night," he said. "Dark, clear, and cool."

"Sounds good to me," Mr. Lipsky said, looking *really* eager. "I'm somewhat of an amateur astronomer myself..."

And Mr. Lipsky went on and on, telling Dad about all the stuff he knew. The rest of us followed behind them, out the cabin door and down onto the lawn.

"So *that's* your dad," Julian said to me as we walked across the grass. "He doesn't look that much like you."

"I look more like my mother," I said. "I mean, my mom and I have the same hair color and stuff."

"Sounds like he knows a *lot* about stars," Blitz said.

"Stars and everything *else* in the universe," I said. "He's an astrophysicist. He works on his science research all the time. He basically just works and sleeps. And drinks coffee."

"Whoa," Julian said. "That's intense."

"*And* he's nocturnal," I added. "Like a bat."

"Cool," Blitz said.

I wouldn't exactly call it *cool*, but whatever.

Once we got to a good open spot on the lawn, Dad said we should all lie on the grass so we didn't wear out our necks looking up at the sky.

And then Dad pointed out the Big Dipper and Cassiopeia, and he showed us how to find the North Star using the Big Dipper's cup as a pointer.

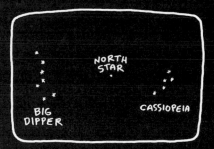

Then Dad showed us Leo the Lion, whose head looks like a backward question mark.

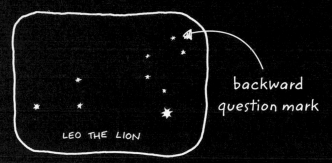

I already knew all those constellations from before (from when I lived in Maryland and Dad and I would look at stars in the yard).

But most of the other kids had grown up in the city, so they'd never really looked at stars like that before. (In the city, the sky looks mostly black with just a few stars here and there.)

Some people were *really* interested. This kid Clarence even pulled out his disposable camera and took a picture of Leo the Lion. I knew the picture wasn't gonna come out, but I didn't say anything, because, well...it just seemed nicer not to.

I have to say, I was kind of glad everyone was having a good time because of my dad.

CHAPTER 7
DR. PARK SAVES THE DAY

The next day at breakfast, we sat with the girls. Dad was still back in the cabin showering, since he's not exactly a morning person. We told the girls all about my Dad's surprise visit, and they told us what they'd found out from talking to Rachel, their cabin counselor.

"So, we talked to Rachel last night," Anika began.

"Did you tell her we heard a voice in Mr. Stark's cabin?" I asked.

"No," Ursula said. "We didn't want her to realize that we'd been snooping around there. That could've been really bad, considering all the rules."

"Exactly," I said.

"We just asked a lot of questions," Anika said. "Like if Mr. Stark's first name was Felix."

"Is it?" Julian asked.

"No," Anika said. "It's *Donald.*"

"So who's Felix?" Blitz asked.

"Who knows," Anika said with a shrug.

"*And* we asked about Mr. Stark's mother," Ursula said. "And Rachel said that Mr. Stark's mother used to live in his cabin till a couple of months ago."

"*Then* what happened?" Blitz asked.

"Well, she was always saying she needed to move somewhere warm, 'cause the winters were too cold for her up here," Anika said. "Apparently she used to complain all the time, to anyone who would listen. Rachel said she was driving Mr. Stark *nuts*."

That didn't sound good.

"So finally, last fall, she got her wish and moved to Arizona," Ursula said.

"To *Arizona*?" Blitz said. "Don't old people usually move to Florida?"

Of course, when Blitz said "Florida," I immediately thought of my dad and the spring-break trip that never happened. But I tried to push that right back out of my mind.

"Arizona's warm, too," Ursula said. "Especially down south in—"

And then Ursula's eyes got enormous.

"PHOENIX!" she burst out. "I bet she moved to *Phoenix*! And I bet *that's* what the voice was saying, not 'Felix'!"

And Ursula jumped up from her seat and went running over to Rachel's table to check out her theory.

"I bet she's right," I said. "The voice was kind of muffled, and it could definitely have been saying 'Phoenix.'"

"Yeah," Julian agreed. "*Ursula* was the one who thought it was 'Felix.' I couldn't really tell."

And sure enough, Ursula came back with a big smile on her face.

"Mr. Stark's mother DID move to Phoenix," she announced proudly.

"But that *still* doesn't tell us who said 'Phoenix' in Mr. Stark's cabin last *night*," Julian pointed out.

"*And* 'gotta get outta here,'" I added.

"*And* 'shut up!'" Sohail added.

We all got quiet.

"Do you think his mother is...still in there?" Julian asked.

"You mean, like, maybe she never really moved?" I asked. "Like everyone here *thinks* she moved, but really she's still there?"

Everyone's face scrunched up as they thought about that one. It didn't seem too likely that Mr. Stark would hide the fact that his mother was still around.

"Or maybe right after she moved, she died, and her ghost came back to haunt the cabin?" Blitz offered.

"Her GHOST?" Ursula said with raised eyebrows. "I don't *think* so."

"But who *else* could it be?" Blitz asked.

"Blitz does have a point," Anika said. "Everyone *says* Mr. Stark lives alone."

"Exactly," Blitz said. "And whoever it is, she's saying the *exact same things* that Mr. Stark's mother used to complain about. So it's definitely connected."

We were all stumped.

"There has to be some kind of logical explanation," Ursula said. "We just have to figure it out..."

✱ ✱ ✱ ✱

But unfortunately, we didn't have *any* time that day to do more investigating, because we were all supposed to go on group hikes out on the nature trails. All of us Spy Fives (and Sohail) got to be in the same hike group together, but we were with my dad, so we couldn't exactly talk openly.

But we *did* decide to ask my dad what he thought of Mr. Stark, just to see if he had any suspicions.

"I think Mr. Stark seems like a very nice man," Dad said. "I talked to him for a while, and I was very impressed. He's really quite an experienced outdoorsman."

"He's a murderer, you know," Ursula said.

"What?" Dad asked, stopping dead in his tracks.

"He kills deer," Ursula explained.

"*Well*, a lot of people do," Dad said. "And it's not such a bad idea. Mr. Stark was telling me that deer populations are growing out of control around here, and there aren't a lot of natural predators to keep the numbers down. I wouldn't call it a crime to help restore balance in the forest."

"Well, *I* think it's cruel," Ursula said.

"How is killing a deer more cruel than killing a chicken or a cow?" Dad asked.

"Those are *farm* animals," Ursula said. "Deer are wild animals."

"Animals are animals," Dad said.

Ursula thought for a moment.

"You can't play by the same rules for every animal," she argued. "They're all different. *We're* animals, and *we're* different."

And so they debated on and on.

The rest of us couldn't take our minds off the voice we'd heard in Mr. Stark's cabin, so we took the opportunity to talk about that.

"I know this might sound crazy," Blitz said, "but maybe Mr. Stark's cabin really *is* haunted. I saw this whole show on TV about haunted houses down in New Orleans and places like that, and people really *do* hear voices."

"I think people make that stuff up," Julian said, shaking his head.

"Why would they do that?" Blitz asked.

"To get people to fork over money to take a tour of their haunted house," Julian said. "*Think* about it. People always wanna make money."

"*That's* for sure," Anika agreed.

"The people on the show really seemed like they believed it," Blitz said with a shrug.

"Maybe they did," I said. "A lot of people *want* to believe that kind of stuff."

"You know what *I* was thinking?" Anika asked. "Maybe there's someone *else* who wanted to go to Phoenix with Mr. Stark's mother. And maybe that person still lives with Mr. Stark. And maybe *that's* whose voice we heard."

"I was thinking something like that," I said.

"But who else could it be?" Julian asked.

"Well, it definitely sounded like a woman's voice," I began.

And then I looked up and realized that my father and Ursula had stopped to wait for us, and that my father had heard me mention the voice.

"What voice?" Dad asked, starting to walk again.

We all got quiet as we followed along.

"Did you hear a voice just now?" Dad asked.

My dad was not one to give up once he started asking about something, so I decided I might as well tell him.

"We heard a voice coming from Mr. Stark's cabin," I said. "We heard it two different times. It said 'Phoenix,' and a couple of other things."

"Who lives with Mr. Stark?" Dad asked.

At that point, we came to a rocky area, so we had to do a little climbing and maneuvering. I could tell my dad was getting tired, because he was running out of breath as he was talking.

"He supposedly lives alone," Ursula said.

"Maybe he talks to himself," Dad suggested. "*I* certainly do."

"Not in *that* voice!" I said.

"What was the voice like?" Dad asked.

"It was high and—" I started to answer, but all of a sudden...

DAD FELL!

He slipped off a rock, landed funny, and crumpled to the ground.

"WHOA!" I said. "DAD!"

"Are you okay?" everyone asked at once.

"I turned my ankle," Dad said, wincing in pain and holding his left foot.

I knelt down beside Dad and looked at his foot. As always, he was wearing his beat-up loafers, which is probably why he slipped. The bottoms were almost completely worn off in parts.

"Can you still walk?" I asked.

"I think it's okay," Dad said, standing up again.

Dad tried to take a few steps, but it was clear that he really couldn't walk.

And that's when Dr. Ursula H. Park sprang into action.

"I know some basic first aid," she said, dropping her backpack on the ground. "I took a training course last summer."

And Ursula opened up her backpack and pulled out a little red first-aid kit.

"You have a FIRST-AID KIT?" Julian asked.

"Yup," Ursula said, unzipping the kit. "I figured I'd bring it to camp, just in case. And sure enough, we need it."

"Girl, you come *prepared*," Anika said, shaking her head in disbelief.

"I'm very impressed," Dad said. "But you shouldn't have to use your first-aid supplies on *me*."

"It's okay," Ursula said. "This is exactly what the supplies are for."

Ursula pulled out a white plastic packet and started squeezing it and shaking it.

"What's that?" Julian asked.

"Instant cold pack," Ursula said. "Activates to 33 degrees Fahrenheit instantly."

"Wow!" Blitz said.

"It's a chemical reaction," Ursula explained.

"Exactly," Dad said, looking impressed.

"Do you think it's a sprain or a break?" Ursula asked my dad. "Did you hear anything snap?"

"Oh, no, definitely not," Dad said. "I'm sure it's just a sprain."

"With sprains, the important thing is to control the swelling right away," Ursula explained, handing the cold pack to my dad. "This'll do the trick. Lasts for thirty minutes. In the meantime, someone should run and get help."

"Me!" Julian said quickly. "I'll go."

"I really don't think you should go alone," Dad said. "You could get lost or hurt, and I'm responsible..."

"I'll go with him," Sohail volunteered. "I know the way...I think."

"I'll go," Anika said quickly. "I *definitely* know the way, and I'm fast."

"You're fast?" Julian asked.

"You better believe it," Anika said, and she took off down the trail in a flash.

"HEY!" Julian and Sohail yelled, chasing after her. "Wait up!"

After Julian, Anika, and Sohail left, the rest of us sat with my dad. Ursula had him raise his ankle to chest level by putting it on a rock. That was supposed to help with the swelling, along with the ice pack. Ursula also gave my dad an elastic bandage and helped him wrap it around his ankle.

"I'm really sorry I ruined the hike," Dad said. "I feel terrible."

"Don't worry," Ursula said. "This made it *especially* interesting."

"Ursula's gonna be a doctor," I explained.

"*And* a lawyer," Ursula added. "But medicine was my first passion."

"I can see that," Dad said.

Then Ursula and my dad talked about the zillion different specialties of medicine that Ursula was considering, all of them huge words ending in "ology."

"I'm hoping Spencer will consider science or medicine, too," Dad said, looking at me.

"No, thanks," I said, rolling my eyes, because Dad was always talking about stuff like that.

He doesn't like it when I say I want to be an artist, or that I'm not really sure (I switch between those two answers).

Fortunately, we didn't have to talk about that stuff for much longer, because Blitz suddenly jumped up.

"HEY!" he yelled. "I hear a motor! Listen!"

And sure enough, we all heard the sound of a motor, getting closer and closer.

And then, suddenly, to our shock, we saw...

SOHAIL BURSTING OVER THE HILL AT THE WHEEL OF AN ATV!

Okay, just kidding. That was Sohail's fantasy version. (I drew it for him.)

In the *real* version, Mr. Stark was at the wheel, and Julian and Sohail were passengers in the back. And they were going a *lot* slower than in Sohail's fantasy version. But Sohail still looked like he was having an awesome time anyway. And so did Julian.

"Nice ride!" Blitz said when the motor went off.

Mr. Stark immediately got off the ATV and went to look at my dad's ankle. Dad kept insisting that it was no big deal and that he was embarrassed by all the special attention.

"It's not a problem," Mr. Stark said.

"Yeah, no problem," Julian agreed.

I could tell that Julian and Sohail were definitely happy to be part of the "special attention." No doubt about that.

"Where's Anika?" I asked Julian.

"There was only enough room for two passengers on the ATV, and she said we could take the spots," Julian said. "She's waiting for us back at the camp."

"We *totally* owe her one," Sohail said. "That was awesome!"

And then he caught himself and said to me:

"I mean, I'm sorry about your dad's ankle."

"It's okay," I said with a shrug, looking at Ursula. "He's gonna be fine, thanks to Dr. Park."

"Anytime," Ursula said with a smile, packing up her first-aid kit.

Mr. Stark helped my dad hobble over to the ATV and sit down in the backseat. (Sohail and Julian had to give up their spots.)

"Now we're going to ride *very slowly* back to camp," Mr. Stark said. "You kids can follow behind us on foot."

And so Mr. Stark drove sloooowly along the trail, and we all walked behind the whole way, listening to Sohail talk about the differences between motorcycles and ATVs, and Julian talk about how fast Anika could run (*really* fast, apparently).

But I, for one, spent a lot of time looking at Mr. Stark as he drove, wondering about the strange voice in his cabin. And I could tell Ursula was thinking about the same thing.

CHAPTER 8
RUBY TALKS TOUGH

When we got to the infirmary, the nurse was totally amazed by Ursula's first-aid job. She said that Ursula had done all the right things, and that Dad would make a quick recovery, thanks to her.

"As long as he keeps icing the ankle," Ursula pointed out. "Thirty minutes on, thirty minutes off."

"Exactly," the nurse said.

"And later tonight, he should use a warm compress," Ursula suggested. "And he might need some painkillers, too."

"Excellent ideas," the nurse said. "Are you sure you're not a doctor already?"

"I'm working on it," Ursula said with a smile.

"Well, good for you, Ursula," Dad said. "Thank you for all your help. I'm very impressed."

And then came the *ultimate* compliment—from Mr. Stark.

"Indeed," Mr. Stark said. "I must say, I'm very impressed, too. *All* of you did very well. You handled the emergency like a team. Great work!"

"Thanks," we all said.

And then Mr. Stark and the nurse talked about getting my dad a pair of crutches so he could get around the camp, and the rest of us started talking amongst ourselves.

"Hey, where's Anika?" Julian asked. "She said she'd meet us here."

"She must've gone back to her cabin or something," Sohail said. "The last time we saw her was outside Mr. Stark's place..."

And then I looked out the window and saw that Anika was out on the lawn in front of the infirmary, walking toward us. When she saw me look out the window, she motioned to me to come outside. She looked really excited.

"*There* she is," I said to the others, pointing out the window. "Let's go."

So we all said we'd be right back and headed outside.

As soon as we stepped out the door, Anika came running up to us.

"GUYS!" she said, barely able to contain her voice in a whisper. "I cracked the case!"

"**YOU DID?**" we all burst out.

"YEAH!" she said. "That's why I gave up my spot on the ATV, 'cause I knew I'd have a chance to peek into Mr. Stark's cabin while he was gone."

"So who was *the voice*?" Ursula interrupted, totally impatient.

"Well, after Mr. Stark left on the ATV with Julian and Sohail, I peeked in the window..."

And that's when the infirmary door opened, and Mr. Stark and my dad came out. Dad was on crutches.

"I'm going to give your father a lift back to his cabin," Mr. Stark said. "We'll just walk over to my place to pick up the golf cart."

"Perfect," Anika said to us with a smile. "Let's go with them, and you can see 'the voice' for yourselves."

And Anika went running up to Mr. Stark, and the rest of us followed.

"Mr. Stark, can we meet Ruby?" Anika asked.

Mr. Stark looked surprised.

"How'd you find out about Ruby?" he asked.

"Rachel told me," she said. "Can we meet her?"

Mr. Stark thought for a second.

"Well, sure, I suppose," he said. "But she'll have to stay in her cage. She can get a little unruly with new people."

Her CAGE? I looked at the others in shock.

And then it dawned on me. Julian, Ursula, and Blitz realized it, too, because we all said, almost at the same time:

"IT'S A BIRD!"

"Exactly," Anika said.

"*Oh!*" Sohail said, smacking his forehead.

"She's a parrot," Mr. Stark explained. "And she's quite a talker."

"So I heard," Anika said, still grinning.

"So *that's* the voice you told me about," Dad said quietly to me.

"Exactly," I said quickly, trying to make sure Dad didn't say anything more, since we didn't want to make it obvious that we'd been spying.

"She's my mother's bird," Mr. Stark explained. "My mother used to live with me, you see. She moved to Arizona last fall, but we couldn't send Ruby with her on the plane. I'm driving Ruby out there next month. And then I'll *finally* get some peace and quiet. I can't *wait*."

"What exactly does the bird say?" Dad asked.

"Oh, too much," Mr. Stark said. "My mother used to talk to her a lot. She used to tell her they were going to move somewhere warm. She even taught her how to say 'Phoenix.'"

"Impressive," Dad said.

Dad didn't even know the *half* of it. I had no idea a bird could say so many different things, and in a voice that sounded so much like a person's! Guess you learn a new thing every day.

✳ ✳ ✳

When we got to Mr. Stark's cabin, we all went inside and met Ruby.

"Hi, Ruby!" we all said.

"**SHUT UP!**" Ruby blasted back.

Mr. Stark winced.

"See, I'm going to be in big trouble for teaching her that!" Mr. Stark said. "That was an accident."

"**SHUT UP!**" Ruby said again.

"She learns language very easily," Mr. Stark explained. "And I got a little frustrated with all her complaining and said some things that I wish—"

"**GOTTA GET OUTTA HERE!**" Ruby interrupted.

"My mother used to say that when she took the cover off of Ruby's cage in the morning," Mr. Stark explained. "She'd say, 'We gotta get outta here, right, Ruby?'"

"**GOTTA GET OUTTA HERE!**" Ruby repeated.

"Just one more month, Ruby," Mr. Stark said, taking a deep breath. "One more month."

"One more month and you can go to Phoenix!" Ursula added.

"**PHOENIX!**" Ruby responded. "**PHOENIX! PHOENIX! PHOENIX!**"

"She definitely knows what she wants, this bird," Mr. Stark said. "And she lets me know. Right, Ruby?"

"**SHUT UP!**" Ruby blasted.

"Now don't say that," Mr. Stark scolded.

And then Ruby said something even *worse*.

We all gasped.

"See?" Mr. Stark said. "When this bird gets to Phoenix, I'm in BIG trouble."

"**PHOENIX!**" Ruby responded. "**PHOENIX! PHOENIX! PHOENIX!**"

It was definitely funny imagining Mr. Stark in trouble with his mom. Ha!

CHAPTER 9
THE HOP-HOP THING

fter we found out about Ruby, we all breathed a major sigh of relief. Everyone was really glad there was nothing creepy about Mr. Stark after all. Well, nothing *too* creepy, that is.

Anyway, after we met Ruby, we all went back to our cabins so we could practice our acts for the talent show.

Julian, Blitz, Sohail, and I did this upside-down head thing I learned when I was at summer camp a few years ago.

We didn't have a lot of time to practice, but still, our act was a huge hit! We did a comedy routine with a bunch of jokes, and everyone really got into it. So that was good.

But what was even *better* was Anika's dance routine. It was AMAZING.

And I'm happy to report that Ursula even figured out the "hop-hop thing." Well, pretty *much*, anyway.

After the talent show, we went on a night hike. Miss Pryor was our group leader, and you could tell she expected everyone to be real scared of being out in the woods in the dark. But not us. After our expedition to Mr. Stark's place, we were like old pros.

Dad stayed behind and helped Mr. Stark get the campfire ready. When we got back, we roasted marshmallows and made s'mores. Then we stayed up really late telling ghost stories and looking at the stars.

The next morning, we all said good-bye to Camp Copper Beech, to all the people and places—including Mr. Stark and the famous copper beech tree itself.

Then everyone got on the buses, and most people were so tired from the night before, they slept the whole way home.

Or at least, that's what I *heard*, because I didn't ride on the bus. I drove back with my dad.

The whole ride back, Dad talked about how we were going to do all this stuff during the summer when I stay with him in Colorado. Like climb some mountain. And raft down some river. So I guess we'll see how that goes.

Oh, and of course Dad *also* spent a lot of the drive explaining to me the latest news on "dark matter." At this point, I think I'm probably the world's youngest expert on the subject. But who knows.

summer plans with Dad?

WELL, AS YOU KNOW, MOST OF THE GALAXY IS INVISIBLE DARK MATTER...

Anyway, another Spy Five operation is all wrapped up, and I'm about ready to turn in for the night. It's Sunday, and tomorrow's our first day back at school after camp.

Exactly thirty-six more school days till SUMMER! (But who's counting?)

Until next time,

Spencer

Spy Gear Manual

Night Vision Headlamp

Red light helps your eyes stay adjusted to the dark.

Use the white light for a bright beam.

Headband keeps your hands free!

Reddy Or Not

Try a test to see if red light really <u>is</u> better for your night vision. Go into a dark room and wait until your eyes are adjusted to the dark so you can see well enough to move around. Then turn on your white light and read a page from a book.

After you turn off the light, do you find it harder to see in the dark? Try the same test with red light and see if your eyes are less "night blind" after you turn off the red light.

Star Power

Spies have to be great navigators, and the stars can help guide the way at night. Want to know how to find north? If you live in the Northern Hemisphere, try this!

1. Look for the Big Dipper in the night sky. It's a very easy-to-find constellation that looks like this:

2. Look at the Dipper's cup. The two stars that form the edge of the cup are the "pointer stars" that point to the North Star.

3. Imagine a line stretching from the two pointers about five times the distance between the two stars. At the end of the line, you'll find the North Star! It's actually a pretty faint little star, but it's an important one. It's always above the North Pole (roughly), so it shows you which way is north.

4. Another way to find the North Star is to look at the constellation Cassiopeia, which looks like a W (or an M). The center of the W (or M) points to the North Star.

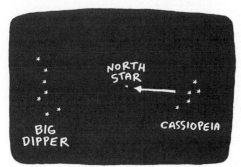

BIG DIPPER

NORTH STAR

CASSIOPEIA

Starry Eyed

Your eyes have to be very adjusted to the dark to really appreciate the stars. That's why astronomers prefer using red light when they have to read notes or star charts. So, when you go outside to check out the stars, make sure to use your red light!

Night Vision Basics for Spies

Wondering why red light is so good for night vision? Here's your answer!

NOT-SO-GOOD NIGHT VISION

GOOD NIGHT VISION

Bright white light causes your iris (the colored part of your eye) to close up to protect your pupil (the black part in the middle of your eye). This means your eyes take in less light, so you won't see very well in the dark right after you turn off the light. Your eyes will need time to readjust.

Red light allows your iris to stay wide open, so your pupil can take in the maximum amount of light.

Have fun... stay cool... be "reddy" for anything ... and you'll be a _stellar_ night spy!
— Spencer